TRAINS

Steaming! *Pulling!* Huffing!

by Patricia Hubbell

illustrated by Megan Halsey and Sean Addy

MARSHALL CAVENDISH

NEW YORK

For Wanda
—P. H.

For the R3 and my NYC
trains, #642 and #172
—M. H.

To my sons
Aidan and Elijah.
And to Tyler, Kendra, and
Jordan. You guys rock!
—S. A.

Marshall Cavendish Corporation
99 White Plains Road, Tarrytown, NY 10591
www.marshallcavendish.us

Text copyright © 2005 by Patricia Hubbell
Illustrations copyright © 2005 by Megan Halsey and Sean Addy

Library of Congress Cataloging-in-Publication Data

Hubbell, Patricia.
Trains : steaming! pulling! huffing! / by Patricia Hubbell ;
illustrated by Megan Halsey and Sean Addy. — 1st ed.
p. cm.
Summary: Rhyming text presents the characteristics of various
kinds of trains.
ISBN 0-7614-5194-3
[1. Railroads—Trains—Fiction. 2. Stories in rhyme.]
I. Halsey, Megan, ill. II. Addy, Sean, ill. III. Title.

PZ8.3.H848Tr 2005
[E]—dc22

2004014468

The text of this book is set in Geometric 415.
The illustrations are rendered in clip art,
etchings, original drawings, and maps.

Book design by Adam Mietlowski

Printed in China

First edition
1 3 5 6 4 2

mc Marshall Cavendish
Children

Trains! Trains! Trains!
Silver trains. Black trains.
Speeding-down-the-track trains.

Welcome to the Prairie State

Land of Lincoln

Passenger trains.

Railway One

Freight trains.

Cowcatcher Express

Welcome to the Bluegrass State

Derby Home

Crossing-every-state trains.

Electric trains.   Diesel trains.

Big old smoky steam trains.

Zoo trains.

Refrigeration Car

Subway trains.

UPTOWN

PENNSYLVANIA STATION

34

Taking-me-to-you trains.

Freights that **rumble**, rock, and **ROAR.**

Quiet Mouse Cheese Co.

Quiet Mouse Cheese Co.

Deep End Pool Supply

Boxcars rolling more . . . and MORE!

Smokestack. Tender. Coupling. Gear.

Red caboose brings up the rear.

Race through valleys.
Climb up ridges.
Whoosh through tunnels.
Cross high bridges.

Giant engines snorting, puffing.

Steaming! Pulling! Rushing! Huffing!

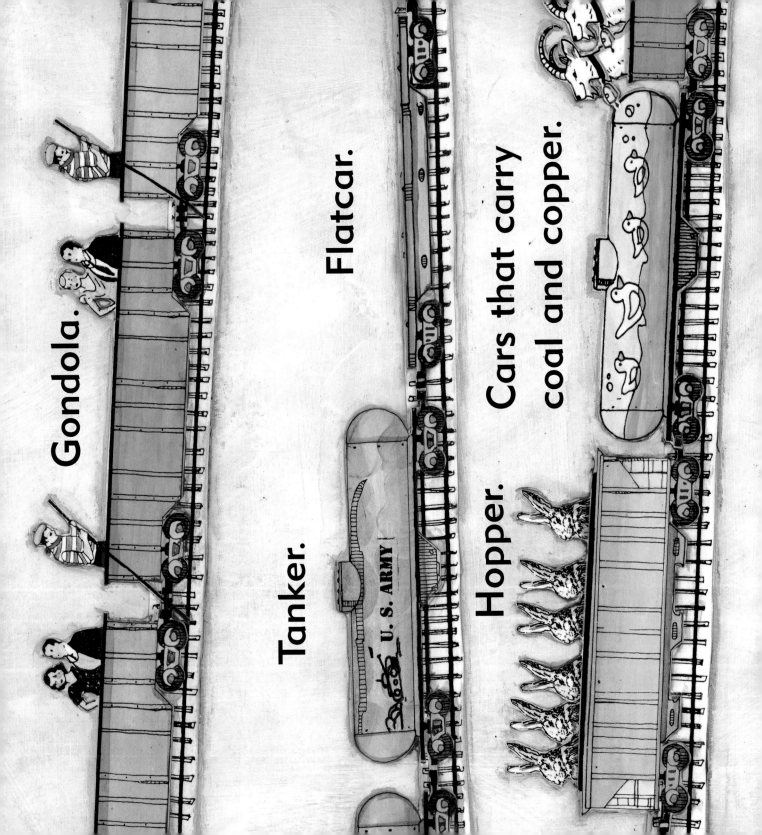

Gondola.

Flatcar.

Tanker.

U. S. ARMY

Hopper.

Cars that carry coal and copper.

Cars that carry ducks 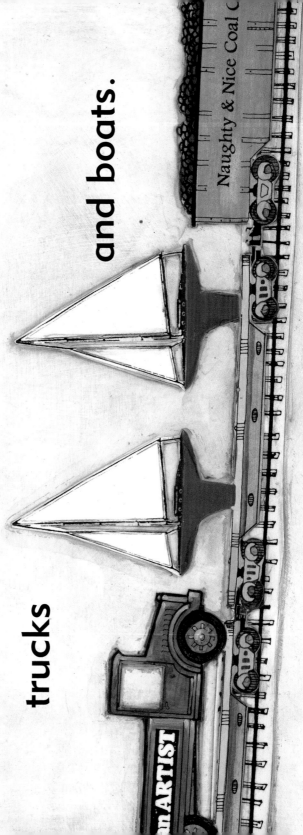 and goats,

milk and oil,

The Gargoyle Oil Corp.

trucks and boats.

Naughty & Nice Coal C

Hissing! Hooting! Rattling! Racketing!

Whooshing! Chugging! Click-clack-clacketing!

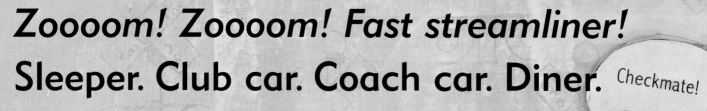

Zoooom! Zoooom! Fast streamliner!
Sleeper. Club car. Coach car. Diner.

Coach Car

Eat at JOE'S

GOOD FOOD

Sleek strong engine, sparkling new!
Dome car's where you see the view.

Greetings from the USA

Have a sandwich. Have a snack. Silver Zephyr's on the track.

Taking folks on their vacation.
All across our great **big** nation.

Trains go dashing through the night.

Tracks lit up by beaming light.

Trains that stop and go and jerk,
take my mom and dad to work.

School
Bus Stop

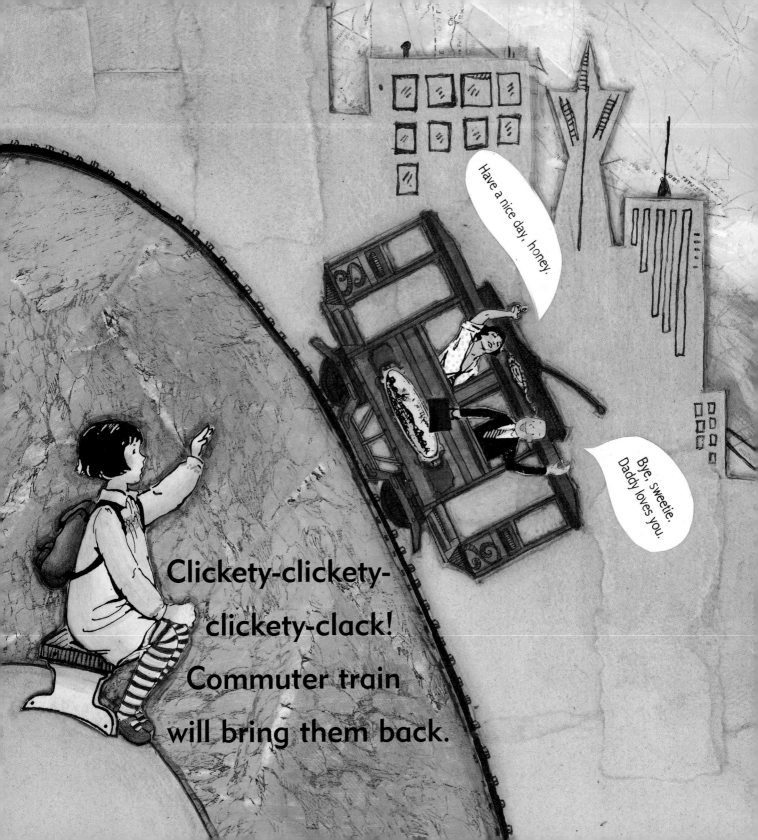

Toy train,
block train,
pulls me fast.

Tooting, hooting,
home at last!

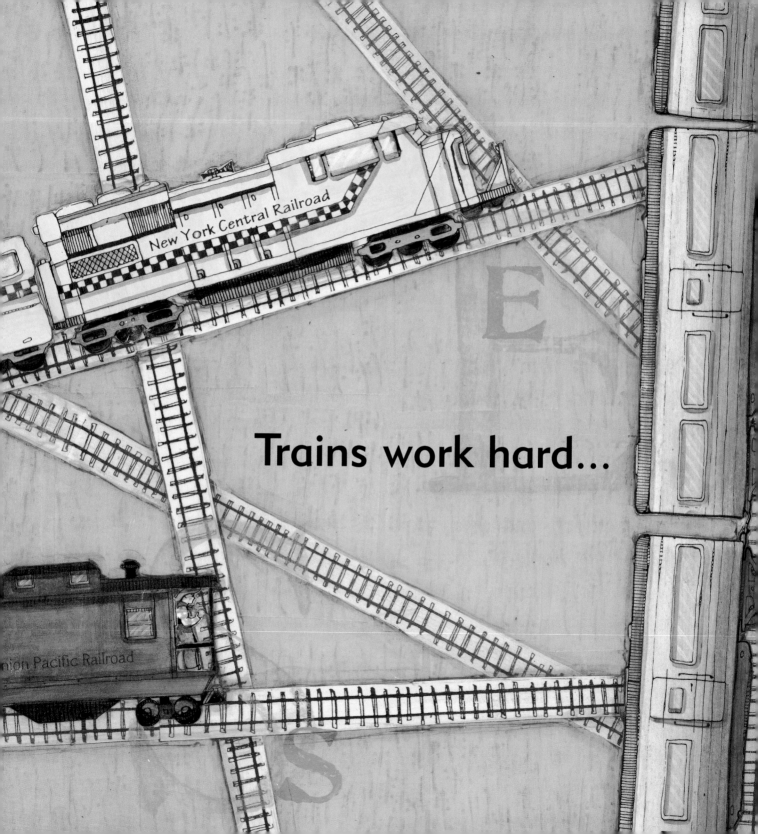

Trains work hard...

...and then they rest.